The Quicksand

Edith Wharton

NOVELLIX
— stories to go —

www.novellix.com

First published in Harpers Magazine, June 1902

Published by Novellix, Stockholm, 2024

Cover image: Shutterstock.com
Cover design: Hanna Hallin
Livonia Print, Riga, 2024
ISBN: 978-91-7589-662-5

MIX
Paper | Supporting responsible forestry
FSC® C002795
FSC
www.fsc.org

I

As Mrs. Quentin's victoria, driving homeward, turned from the Park into Fifth Avenue, she divined her son's tall figure walking ahead of her in the twilight. His long stride covered the ground more rapidly than usual, and she had a premonition that, if he were going home at that hour, it was because he wanted to see her.

Mrs. Quentin, though not a fanciful woman, was sometimes aware of a sixth sense enabling her to detect the faintest vibrations of her son's impulses. She was too shrewd to fancy herself the one mother in possession of this faculty, but she permitted herself to think that few could exercise it more discreetly. If she could not help overhearing Alan's thoughts, she had the courage to keep her discoveries to herself, the tact to take for granted nothing that lay below the surface of their spoken intercourse: she knew that most people would rather have their letters read than their thoughts. For this superfeminine discretion Alan repaid her by – being Alan. There could have been no completer reward. He was the key to the meaning of life, the justification of what must have seemed as incomprehensible as it was odious, had it not all-sufficingly ended in himself. He was a perfect son, and Mrs. Quentin had always hungered for perfection.

Her house, in a minor way, bore witness to the craving. One felt it to be the result of a series of eliminations: there was nothing fortuitous in its blending of line and color. The almost morbid finish of every material detail of her life suggested the possibility that a diversity of energies had, by some pressure of circumstance, been forced into the channel of a narrow dilettanteism. Mrs. Quentin's fastidiousness had, indeed, the flaw of being too one sided. Her friends were not always worthy of the chairs they sat in, and she overlooked in her associates defects she would not have tolerated in her bric-a-brac. Her house was, in fact, never so distinguished as when it was empty; and it was at its best in the warm fire-lit silence that now received her.

Her son, who had overtaken her on the doorstep, followed her into the drawing room, and threw himself into an armchair near the fire, while she laid off her furs and busied herself about the tea table. For a while neither spoke; but glancing at him across the kettle, his mother noticed that he sat staring at the embers with a look she had never seen on his face, though its arrogant young outline was as familiar to her as her own thoughts. The look extended itself to his negligent attitude, to the droop of his long fine hands, the dejected tilt of his head against the cushions. It was like the moral equivalent of physical fatigue: he looked, as he himself would have phrased it, dead-beat, played out. Such an air was so foreign to his usual bright indomitableness that Mrs. Quentin had the sense of an unfamiliar presence, in which she must observe herself, must raise hurried barriers against an alien approach. It was one of the drawbacks of their excessive intimacy that any break in it seemed a chasm.

She was accustomed to let his thoughts circle about her before they settled into speech, and she now sat in motionless expectancy, as though a sound might frighten them away.

At length, without turning his eyes from the fire, he said: "I'm so glad you're a nice old-fashioned intuitive woman. It's painful to see them think."

Her apprehension had already preceded him. "Hope Fenno–?" she faltered.

He nodded. "She's been thinking – hard. It was very painful – to me, at least; and I don't believe she enjoyed it: she said she didn't." He stretched his feet to the fire. "The result of her cogitations is that she won't have me. She arrived at this by pure ratiocination – it's not a question of feeling, you understand. I'm the only man she's ever loved – but she won't have me. What novels did you read when you were young, dear? I'm convinced it all turns on that. If she'd been brought up on Trollope and Whyte-Melville, instead of Tolstoi and Mrs. Ward, we should have now been vulgarly sitting on a sofa, trying on the engagement ring."

Mrs. Quentin at first was kept silent by the mother's instinctive anger that the girl she has not wanted for her son should have dared to refuse him. Then she said, "Tell me, dear."

"My good woman, she has scruples."

"Scruples?"

"Against the paper. She objects to me in my official capacity as owner of the *Radiator*."

His mother did not echo his laugh.

"She had found a solution, of course – she overflows with expedients. I was to chuck the paper, and we were to live happily ever afterward on canned food and virtue. She even had an alternative ready – women are so full of resources! I was to turn the *Radiator* into an independent organ, and run it at a loss to show the public what a model newspaper ought to be. On the whole, I think she fancied this plan more than the other – it commended itself to her as being more uncomfortable and aggressive. It's not the fashion nowadays to be good by stealth."

Mrs. Quentin said to herself, "I didn't know how much he cared!" Aloud she murmured, "You must give her time."

"Time?"

"To move out the old prejudices and make room for new ones."

"My dear mother, those she has are brand-new; that's the trouble with them. She's tremendously up-to-date. She takes in all the moral fashion-papers, and wears the newest thing in ethics."

Her resentment lost its way in the intricacies of his metaphor. "Is she so very religious?"

"You dear archaic woman! She's hopelessly irreligious; that's the difficulty. You can make a religious woman believe almost anything: there's the habit of credulity to work on. But when a girl's faith in the Deluge has been shaken, it's very hard to inspire her with confidence. She makes you feel that, before believing in you, it's her duty as a conscientious agnostic to find out whether you're not obsolete, or whether the text isn't corrupt, or somebody hasn't proved conclusively that you never existed, anyhow."

Mrs. Quentin was again silent. The two moved in

that atmosphere of implications and assumptions where the lightest word may shake down the dust of countless stored impressions; and speech was sometimes more difficult between them than had their union been less close.

Presently she ventured, "It's impossible?"

"Impossible?"

She seemed to use her words cautiously, like weapons that might slip and inflict a cut. "What she suggests."

Her son, raising himself, turned to look at her for the first time. Their glance met in a shock of comprehension. He was with her against the girl, then! Her satisfaction overflowed in a murmur of tenderness.

"Of course not, dear. One can't change – change one's life …"

"One's self," he emended. "That's what I tell her. What's the use of my giving up the paper if I keep my point of view?"

The psychological distinction attracted her. "Which is it she minds most?"

"Oh, the paper – for the present. She undertakes to modify the point of view afterward. All she asks is that I shall renounce my heresy: the gift of grace will come later."

Mrs. Quentin sat gazing into her untouched cup. Her son's first words had produced in her the hallucinated sense of struggling in the thick of a crowd that he could not see. It was horrible to feel herself hemmed in by influences imperceptible to him; yet if anything could have increased her misery it would have been the discovery that her ghosts had become visible.

As though to divert his attention, she precipitately asked, "And you–?"

His answer carried the shock of an evocation. "I merely asked her what she thought of you."

"Of me?"

"She admires you immensely, you know."

For a moment Mrs. Quentin's cheek showed the lingering light of girlhood: praise transmitted by her son acquired something of the transmitter's merit. "Well–?" she smiled.

"Well – you didn't make my father give up the *Radiator*, did you?"

His mother, stiffening, made a circuitous return: "She never comes here. How can she know me?"

"She's so poor! She goes out so little." He rose and leaned against the mantelpiece, dislodging with impatient fingers a slender bronze wrestler poised on a porphyry base, between two warm toned Spanish ivories. "And then her mother–" he added, as if involuntarily.

"Her mother has never visited me," Mrs. Quentin finished for him.

He shrugged his shoulders. "Mrs. Fenno has the

scope of a wax doll. Her rule of conduct is taken from her grandmother's sampler."

"But the daughter is so modern – and yet –"

"The result is the same? Not exactly. *She* admires you – oh, immensely!" He replaced the bronze and turned to his mother with a smile. "Aren't you on some hospital committee together? What especially strikes her is your way of doing good. She says philanthropy is not a line of conduct, but a state of mind – and it appears that you are one of the elect."

As, in the vague diffusion of physical pain, relief seems to come with the acuter pang of a single nerve, Mrs. Quentin felt herself suddenly eased by a rush of anger against the girl. "If she loved you–" she began.

His gesture checked her. "I'm not asking you to get her to do that."

The two were again silent, facing each other in the disarray of a common catastrophe – as though their thoughts, at the summons of danger, had rushed naked into action. Mrs. Quentin, at this revealing moment, saw for the first time how many elements of her son's character had seemed comprehensible simply because they were familiar: as, in reading a foreign language, we take the meaning of certain words for granted till the context corrects us. Often as in a given case, her maternal musings had figured his conduct, she now found herself at a loss to forecast it;

and with this failure of intuition came a sense of the subserviency which had hitherto made her counsels but the anticipation of his wish. Her despair escaped in the moan, "What *is* it you ask me?"

"To talk to her."

"Talk to her?"

"Show her – tell her – make her understand that the paper has always been a thing outside your life – that hasn't touched you – that needn't touch her. Only, let her hear you – watch you – be with you – she'll see … she can't help seeing …"

His mother faltered. "But if she's given you her reasons–?"

"Let her give them to you! If she can – when she sees you …" His impatient hand again displaced the wrestler. "I care abominably," he confessed.

II

On the Fenno threshold a sudden sense of the futility of the attempt had almost driven Mrs. Quentin back to her carriage; but the door was already opening, and a parlor-maid who believed that Miss Fenno was in led the way to the depressing drawing-room. It was the kind of room in which no member of the family is likely to be found except after dinner or after death. The chairs and tables looked like poor relations who had repaid their keep by a long career of grudging usefulness: they seemed banded together against intruders in a sullen conspiracy of discomfort. Mrs. Quentin, keenly susceptible to such influences, read failure in every angle of the upholstery. She was incapable of the vulgar error of thinking that Hope Fenno might be induced to marry Alan for his money; but between this assumption and the inference that the girl's imagination might be touched by the finer possibilities of wealth, good taste admitted a distinction. The Fenno furniture, however, presented to such reasoning the obtuseness of its black walnut chamferings; and something in its attitude suggested that its owners would be as uncompromising. The room showed none of the modern attempts at palliation, no apologetic draping of facts; and Mrs. Quentin, provisionally perched on a green reps Gothic sofa with which it was clearly impossible to establish any closer relations, concluded that, had Mrs. Fenno needed another seat of the same size, she would have set out placidly to match the one on which her visitor now languished.

To Mrs. Quentin's fancy, Hope Fenno's opinions, presently imparted in a clear young voice from the opposite angle of the Gothic sofa, partook of the character of their surroundings. The girl's mind was like a large light empty place, scantily furnished with a few massive prejudices, not designed to add to any one's comfort but too ponderous to be easily moved. Mrs. Quentin's own intelligence, in which its owner, in an artistically shaded half light, had so long moved amid a delicate complexity of sensations, seemed in comparison suddenly close and crowded; and in taking refuge there from the glare of the young girl's candor, the older woman found herself stumbling in an unwonted obscurity. Her uneasiness resolved itself into a sense of irritation against her listener. Mrs. Quentin knew that the momentary value of any argument lies in the capacity of the mind to which it is addressed, and as her shafts of persuasion spent themselves against Miss Fenno's obduracy, she said to herself that, since conduct is governed by emotions rather than ideas, the really strong people are those who mistake their sensations for opinions. Viewed in this light, Miss Fenno was certainly very strong: there was an unmistakable ring of finality in the tone with which she declared,

"It's impossible."

Mrs. Quentin's answer veiled the least shade of feminine resentment. "I told Alan that, where he had failed, there was no chance of my making an impression."

Hope Fenno laid on her visitor's an almost reverential hand. "Dear Mrs. Quentin, it's the impression you make that confirms the impossibility."

Mrs. Quentin waited a moment: she was perfectly

aware that, where her feelings were concerned, her sense of humor was not to be relied on. "Do I make such an odious impression?" she asked at length, with a smile that seemed to give the girl her choice of two meanings.

"You make such a beautiful one! It's too beautiful – it obscures my judgment."

Mrs. Quentin looked at her thoughtfully. "Would it be permissible, I wonder, for an older woman to suggest that, at your age, it isn't always a misfortune to have what one calls one's judgment temporarily obscured?"

Miss Fenno flushed. "I try not to judge others–"

"You judge Alan."

"Ah, *he* is not others," she murmured, with an accent that touched the older woman.

"You judge his mother."

"I don't; I don't!"

Mrs. Quentin pressed her point. "You judge yourself, then, as you would be in my position – and your verdict condemns me."

"How can you think it? It's because I appreciate the difference in our point of view that I find it so difficult to defend myself–"

"Against what?"

"The temptation to imagine that I might be as you are – feeling as I do."

Mrs. Quentin rose with a sigh. "My child, in my day love was less subtle." She added, after a moment, "Alan is a perfect son."

"Ah, that again – that makes it worse!"

"Worse?"

"Just as your goodness does, your sweetness, your immense indulgence in letting me discuss things with you in a way that must seem almost an impertinence."

Mrs. Quentin's smile was not without irony. "You must remember that I do it for Alan."

"That's what I love you for!" the girl instantly returned; and again her tone touched her listener.

"And yet you're sacrificing him – and to an idea!"

"Isn't it to ideas that all the sacrifices that were worth while have been made?"

"One may sacrifice one's self."

Miss Fenno's color rose. "That's what I'm doing," she said gently.

Mrs. Quentin took her hand. "I believe you are," she answered. "And it isn't true that I speak only for Alan. Perhaps I did when I began; but now I want to plead for you too – against yourself." She paused, and then went on with a deeper note: "I have let you, as you say, speak your mind to me in terms that some women might have resented, because I wanted to show you how little, as the years go on, theories, ideas, abstract conceptions of life, weigh against the actual, against the particular way in which life presents itself to us – to women especially. To decide beforehand exactly how one ought to behave in given circumstances is like deciding that one will follow a certain direction in crossing an unexplored country. Afterward we find that we must turn out for the obstacles – cross the rivers where they're shallowest – take the tracks that others have beaten – make all sorts of unexpected concessions. Life is made up of compromises: that is what youth refuses to understand. I've lived long enough to doubt whether any real good ever came of sacrificing beautiful facts to even more beautiful theories. Do I seem casuistical? I don't know – there may be losses either way… but the love of the man one loves… of the child one loves… that makes up for everything…."

She had spoken with a thrill which seemed to communicate itself to the hand her listener had left in hers. Her eyes filled suddenly, but through their dimness she saw the girl's lips shape a last desperate denial:

"Don't you see it's because I feel all this that I mustn't – that I can't?"

III

Mrs. Quentin, in the late spring afternoon, had turned in at the doors of the Metropolitan Museum. She had been walking in the Park, in a solitude oppressed by the ever-present sense of her son's trouble, and had suddenly remembered that some one had added a Beltraffio to the collection. It was an old habit of Mrs. Quentin's to seek in the enjoyment of the beautiful the distraction that most of her acquaintances appeared to find in each other's company. She had few friends, and their society was welcome to her only in her more superficial moods; but she could drug anxiety with a picture as some women can soothe it with a bonnet.

During the six months that had elapsed since her visit to Miss Fenno she had been conscious of a pain of which she had supposed herself no longer capable: as a man will continue to feel the ache of an amputated arm. She had fancied that all her centres of feeling had been transferred to Alan; but she now found herself subject to a kind of dual suffering, in which her individual pang was the keener in that it divided her from her son's. Alan had surprised her: she had not foreseen that he would take a sentimental rebuff so hard. His disappointment took the uncommunicative form of a sterner application to work. He threw himself into the concerns of the *Radiator* with an aggressiveness that almost betrayed itself in the paper. Mrs. Quentin never read the *Radiator*, but from the glimpses of it reflected in the other journals she gathered that it was at least not being subjected to the moral reconstruction which had been one of Miss Fenno's alternatives.

Mrs. Quentin never spoke to her son of what had happened. She was superior to the cheap satisfaction of avenging his injury by depreciating its cause. She knew that in sentimental sorrows such consolations are as salt in the wound. The avoidance of a subject so vividly present to both could not but affect the closeness of their relation. An invisible presence hampered their liberty of speech and thought. The girl was always between them; and to hide the sense of her intrusion they began to be less frequently together. It was then that Mrs. Quentin measured the extent of her isolation. Had she ever dared to forecast such a situation, she would have proceeded on the conventional theory that her son's suffering must draw her nearer to him; and this was precisely the relief that was denied her. Alan's uncommunicativeness extended below the level of speech, and his mother, reduced to the helplessness of dead reckoning, had not even the solace of adapting her sympathy to his needs. She did not know what he felt: his course was incalculable to her. She sometimes wondered if she had become as incomprehensible to him; and it was to find a moment's refuge from the dogging misery of such conjectures that she had now turned in at the Museum.

The long line of mellow canvases seemed to receive her into the rich calm of an autumn twilight. She might have been walking in an enchanted wood where the footfall of care never sounded. So deep was the sense of seclusion that, as she turned from her prolonged communion with the new Beltraffio, it was a surprise to find she was not alone.

A young lady who had risen from the central ottoman stood in suspended flight as Mrs. Quentin faced her. The older woman was the first to regain her self-possession.

"Miss Fenno!" she said.

The girl advanced with a blush. As it faded, Mrs. Quentin noticed a change in her. There had always been something bright and bannerlike in her aspect, but now her look drooped, and she hung at half-mast, as it were. Mrs. Quentin, in the embarrassment of surprising a secret that its possessor was doubtless unconscious of betraying, reverted hurriedly to the Beltraffio.

"I came to see this," she said. "It's very beautiful."

Miss Fenno's eye travelled incuriously over the mystic blue reaches of the landscape. "I suppose so," she assented; adding, after another tentative pause, "You come here often, don't you?"

"Very often," Mrs. Quentin answered. "I find pictures a great help."

"A help?"

"A rest, I mean ... if one is tired or out of sorts."

"Ah," Miss Fenno murmured, looking down.

"This Beltraffio is new, you know," Mrs. Quentin continued. "What a wonderful background, isn't it? Is he a painter who interests you?"

The girl glanced again at the dusky canvas, as though in a final endeavor to extract from it a clue to the consolations of art. "I don't know," she said at length; "I'm afraid I don't understand pictures." She moved nearer to Mrs. Quentin and held out her hand.

"You're going?"

"Yes."

Mrs. Quentin looked at her. "Let me drive you home," she said, impulsively. She was feeling, with a shock of surprise, that it gave her, after all, no pleasure to see how much the girl had suffered.

Miss Fenno stiffened perceptibly. "Thank you; I shall like the walk."

Mrs. Quentin dropped her hand with a corresponding movement of withdrawal, and a momentary wave of antagonism seemed to sweep the two women apart. Then, as Mrs. Quentin, bowing slightly, again addressed herself to the picture, she felt a sudden touch on her arm.

"Mrs. Quentin," the girl faltered, "I really came here because I saw your carriage." Her eyes sank, and then fluttered back to her hearer's face. "I've been horribly unhappy!" she exclaimed.

Mrs. Quentin was silent. If Hope Fenno had expected an immediate response to her appeal, she was disappointed. The older woman's face was like a veil dropped before her thoughts.

"I've thought so often," the girl went on precipitately, "of what you said that day you came to see me last autumn. I think I understand now what you mean – what you tried to make me see... Oh, Mrs. Quentin," she broke out, "I didn't mean to tell you this – I never dreamed of it till this moment – but you do remember what you said, don't you? You must *remember* it! And now that I've met you in this way, I can't help telling you that I believe – I begin to believe – that you were right, after all."

Mrs. Quentin had listened without moving; but now she raised her eyes with a slight smile. "Do you wish me to say this to Alan?" she asked.

The girl flushed, but her glance braved the smile. "Would he still care to hear it?" she said fearlessly.

Mrs. Quentin took momentary refuge in a renewed inspection of the Beltraffio; then, turning, she said, with a kind of reluctance: "He would still care."

"Ah!" broke from the girl.

During this exchange of words the two speakers had drifted unconsciously toward one of the benches.

Mrs. Quentin glanced about her: a custodian who had been hovering in the doorway sauntered into the adjoining gallery, and they remained alone among the silvery Vandykes and flushed bituminous Halses. Mrs. Quentin sank down on the bench and reached a hand to the girl.

"Sit by me," she said.

Miss Fenno dropped beside her. In both women the stress of emotion was too strong for speech. The girl was still trembling, and Mrs. Quentin was the first to regain her composure.

"You say you've suffered," she began at last. "Do you suppose *I* haven't?"

"I knew you had. That made it so much worse for me – that I should have been the cause of your suffering for Alan!"

Mrs. Quentin drew a deep breath. "Not for Alan only," she said. Miss Fenno turned on her a wondering glance. "Not for Alan only. That pain every woman expects – and knows how to bear. We all know our children must have such disappointments, and to suffer with them is not the deepest pain. It's the suffering apart – in ways they don't understand." She breathed deeply. "I want you to know what I mean. You were right – that day – and I was wrong."

"Oh," the girl faltered.

Mrs. Quentin went on in a voice of passionate lucidity. "I knew it then – I knew it even while I was trying to argue with you – I've always known it! I didn't want my son to marry you till I heard your reasons for refusing him; and then – then I longed to see you his wife!"

"Oh, Mrs. Quentin!"

"I longed for it; but I knew it mustn't be."

"Mustn't be?"

Mrs. Quentin shook her head sadly, and the girl, gaining courage from this mute negation, cried with an uncontrollable escape of feeling:

"It's because you thought me hard, obstinate narrow-minded? Oh, I understand that so well! My self-righteousness must have seemed so petty! A girl who could sacrifice a man's future to her own moral vanity – for it was a form of vanity; you showed me that plainly enough – how you must have despised me! But I am not that girl now – indeed I'm not. I'm not impulsive – I think things out. I've thought this out. I know Alan loves me – I know *how* he loves me – and I believe I can help him – oh, not in the ways I had fancied before – but just merely by loving him." She paused, but Mrs. Quentin made no sign. "I see it all so differently now. I see what an influence love itself may be – how my believing in him, loving him, accepting him just as he is, might help him more than any theories, any arguments. I might have seen this long ago in looking at you – as he often told me – in seeing how you'd kept yourself apart from – from – Mr. Quentin's work and his – been always the beautiful side of life to them – kept their faith alive in spite of themselves – not by interfering, preaching, reforming, but by – just loving them and being there–" She looked at Mrs. Quentin with a simple nobleness. "It isn't as if I cared for the money, you know; if I cared for that, I should be afraid–"

"You will care for it in time," Mrs. Quentin said suddenly.

Miss Fenno drew back, releasing her hand. "In time?"

"Yes; when there's nothing else left." She stared a moment at the pictures. "My poor child," she broke out, "I've heard all you say so often before!"

"You've heard it?"

"Yes – from myself. I felt as you do, I argued as you do, I acted as I mean to prevent your doing, when I married Alan's father."

The long empty gallery seemed to reverberate with the girl's startled exclamation– "Oh, Mrs. Quentin–"

"Hush; let me speak. Do you suppose I'd do this if you were the kind of pink-and-white idiot he ought to have married? It's because I see you're alive, as I was, tingling with beliefs, ambitions, energies, as I was – that I can't see you walled up alive, as I was, without stretching out a hand to save you!" She sat gazing rigidly forward, her eyes on the pictures, speaking in the low precipitate tone of one who tries to press the meaning of a lifetime into a few breathless sentences.

"When I met Alan's father," she went on, "I knew nothing of his – his work. We met abroad, where I had been living with my mother. That was twenty-six years ago, when the *Radiator* was less – less notorious than it is now. I knew my husband owned a newspaper – a great newspaper – and nothing more. I had never seen a copy of the *Radiator*; I had no notion what it stood for, in politics – or in other ways. We were married in Europe, and a few months afterward we came to live here. People were already beginning to talk about the *Radiator*. My husband, on leaving college, had bought it with some money an old uncle had left him, and the public at first was merely curious to see what an ambitious, stirring young man without any experience of journalism was going to make out of his experiment. They found first of all that he was going to make a great deal of money out of it. I found that out too. I was so happy in other ways that it didn't make much difference at first; though it was pleasant to be able to help my mother, to be generous and charitable, to live in a nice house, and wear the handsome gowns he liked to see me in. But still it didn't really count – it counted so little that when, one day, I learned what the *Radiator* was, I would have gone out into the streets barefooted rather than live another hour on the money it brought in…" Her voice sank, and she paused to steady it. The girl at her side did not speak or move. "I shall never forget that day," she began again. "The paper had stripped bare some family scandal – some miserable bleeding secret that a dozen unhappy people had been struggling to keep out of print – that would have been kept out if my husband had not – Oh, you must guess the rest! I can't go on!"

She felt a hand on hers. "You mustn't go on, Mrs. Quentin," the girl whispered.

"Yes, I must – I must! You must be made to understand." She drew a deep breath. "My husband was not like Alan. When he found out how I felt about it he was surprised at first – but gradually he began to see – or at least I fancied he saw – the hatefulness of it. At any rate he saw how I suffered, and he offered to give up the whole thing – to sell the paper. It couldn't be done all of a sudden, of course – he made me see that – for he had put all his money in it, and he had no special aptitude for any other kind of work. He was a born journalist – like Alan. It was a great sacrifice for him to give up the paper, but he promised to do it – in time – when a good opportunity offered. Meanwhile, of course, he wanted to build it up, to increase the circulation – and to do that he had to keep on in the same way – he made that clear to me. I saw that we were in a vicious circle. The paper, to sell well, had to be made more and more detestable and disgraceful. At first I rebelled – but somehow – I can't tell you how it was – after that first concession the ground seemed to give under me: with every struggle I sank deeper. And then – then Alan was born. He was such a delicate baby that there was very little hope of saving him. But money did it – the money from the paper. I took him abroad to see the best physicians – I took him to a warm climate every winter. In hot weather the doctors recommended sea air, and we had a yacht and cruised every summer. I owed his life to the *Radiator*. And when he began to grow stronger the habit was formed—the habit of luxury. He could not get on without the things he had always been used to. He pined in bad air; he drooped under monotony and discomfort; he throve on variety, amusement, travel, every kind of novelty and excitement. And all I wanted for him his inexhaustible foster-mother was there to give!

"My husband said nothing, but he must have seen how things were going. There was no more talk of giving up the *Radiator*. He never reproached me with my inconsistency, but I thought he must despise me, and the thought made me reckless. I determined to ignore the paper altogether – to take what it gave as though I didn't know where it came from. And to excuse this I invented the theory that one may, so to speak, purify money by putting it to good uses. I gave away a great deal in charity – I indulged myself very little at first. All the money that was not spent on Alan I tried to do good with. But gradually, as my boy grew up, the problem became more complicated. How was I to protect Alan from the contamination I had let him live in? I couldn't preach by example – couldn't hold up his father as a warning, or denounce the money we were living on. All I could do was to disguise the inner ugliness of life by making it beautiful outside – to build a wall of beauty between him and the facts of life, turn his tastes and interests another way, hide the *Radiator* from him as a smiling woman at a ball may hide a cancer in her breast! Just as Alan was entering college his father died. Then I saw my way clear. I had loved my husband – and yet I drew my first free breath in years. For the *Radiator* had been left to Alan outright – there was nothing on earth to prevent his selling it when he came of age. And there was no excuse for his not selling it. I had brought him up to depend on money, but the paper had given us enough money to gratify all his tastes. At last we could turn on the monster that had nourished us. I felt a savage joy in the thought –

I could hardly bear to wait till Alan came of age. But I had never spoken to him of the paper, and I didn't dare speak of it now. Some false shame kept me back, some vague belief in his ignorance. I would wait till he was twenty-one, and then we should be free.

"I waited – the day came, and I spoke. You can guess his answer, I suppose. He had no idea of selling the *Radiator*. It wasn't the money he cared for – it was the career that tempted him. He was a born journalist, and his ambition, ever since he could remember, had been to carry on his father's work, to develop, to surpass it. There was nothing in the world as interesting as modern journalism. He couldn't imagine any other kind of life that wouldn't bore him to death. A newspaper like the *Radiator* might be made one of the biggest powers on earth, and he loved power, and meant to have all he could get. I listened to him in a kind of trance. I couldn't find a word to say. His father had had scruples – he had none. I seemed to realize at once that argument would be useless. I don't know that I even tried to plead with him – he was so bright and hard and inaccessible! Then I saw that he was, after all, what I had made him – the creature of my concessions, my connivances, my evasions. That was the price I had paid for him – I had kept him at that cost!

"Well – I *had* kept him, at any rate. That was the

feeling that survived. He was my boy, my son, my very own – till some other woman took him. Meanwhile the old life must go on as it could. I gave up the struggle. If at that point he was inaccessible, at others he was close to me. He has always been a perfect son. Our tastes grew together – we enjoyed the same books, the same pictures, the same people. All I had to do was to look at him in profile to see the side of him that was really mine. At first I kept thinking of the dreadful other side – but gradually the impression faded, and I kept my mind turned from it, as one does from a deformity in a face one loves. I thought I had made my last compromise with life – had hit on a *modus vivendi* that would last my time.

"And then he met you. I had always been prepared for his marrying, but not a girl like you. I thought he would choose a sweet thing who would never pry into his closets – he hated women with ideas! But as soon as I saw you I knew the struggle would have to begin again. He is so much stronger than his father – he is full of the most monstrous convictions. And he has the courage of them, too – you saw last year that his love for you never made him waver. He believes in his work; he adores it – it is a kind of hideous idol to which he would make human sacrifices! He loves you still – I've been honest with you – but his love wouldn't change him. It is you who would have to change – to die gradually, as I have died, till there is only one live point left in me. Ah, if one died completely – that's simple enough! But something persists – remember that – a single point, an aching nerve of truth. Now and then you may drug it – but a touch wakes it again, as your face has waked it in me. There's always enough of one's old self left to suffer with …"

She stood up and faced the girl abruptly. "What shall I tell Alan?" she said.

Miss Fenno sat motionless, her eyes on the ground. Twilight was falling on the gallery – a twilight which seemed to emanate not so much from the glass dome overhead as from the crepuscular depths into which the faces of the pictures were receding. The custodian's step sounded warningly down the corridor. When the girl looked up she was alone.

SHORT STORIES PUBLISHED BY NOVELLIX

N°1 Virginia Woolf *Lappin and Lapinova*
N°2 D.H. Lawrence *Sun*
N°3 Katherine Mansfield *Bliss*
N°4 Charles Dickens *Horatio Sparkins*
N°5 Astrid Lindgren *Most Beloved Sister & Mirabelle*
N°6 August Strindberg *Frictions*
N°7 Selma Lagerlöf *The Silver Mine*
N°8 Stig Dagerman *Sleet*
N°9 Håkan Nesser *How I Spend My Days and My Nights*
N°10 Karin Tidbeck *Anywhere Out of the World*
N°11 Arne Dahl *Migraine*
N°12 Henning Mankell *The Man on the Beach*
N°13 Oscar Wilde *The Nightinggale and the Rose…*
N°14 Mary Shelley *The Trial of Love*
N°15 Leo Tolstoy *After the Dance*
N°16 Virginia Woolf *The Legacy*
N°17 Karen Blixen *The Pearls*
N°18 Henrik Pontoppidan *The Grim Reaper*
N°19 Herman Bang *Irene Holm*
N°20 H.C. Andersen *Little Claus and Big Claus*
N°21 Selma Lagerlöf *The Legend of the Christmas Rose*
N°22 Charles Dickens *A Christmas Carol – Stave one*
N°23 Louisa May Alcott *A Christmas Dream*
N°24 H.C. Andersen *The Fir Tree*
N°25 Virginia Woolf *Kew Gardens*
N°26 James Joyce *The Boarding House*
N°27 Edith Wharton *The Quicksand*
N°28 Katherine Mansfield *The Garden Party*